TIME TOGETHER
Me and Mom

BY MARIA CATHERINE
ILLUSTRATED BY PASCAL CAMPION

PICTURE WINDOW BOOKS

THIS BOOK BELONGS TO:

- -

Cozy cuddle time

Tasty cooking time

Carefree summer time

Splish splash
bubble time

What-to-wear time

Food adventure time

Creative quiet time

Fly high time

Squeeze tight time

Beauty salon time

Chugga-chugga choo-choo time

Secret sharing time

Sweet dream time

Time Together is published by Picture Window Books
A Capstone Imprint
1710 Roe Crest Drive
North Mankato, Minnesota 56003
www.capstonepub.com

Library of Congress Cataloging-in-Publication data
is available on the Library of Congress website.
ISBN: 978-1-4795-2252-1 (paper over board)
ISBN: 978-1-4795-2254-5 (paperback)

Summary:
Snapshots of a mom and child enjoying
every day moments together.

Concepted by:
Kay Fraser and Christianne Jones

Designer:
K. Fraser

Photo Credit:
Shutterstock

Printed in Canada.
052014   008235R